CLEMENTINE ROSE

and the Pet Day Disaster

Books by Jacqueline Harvey

Clementine Rose and the Surprise Visitor
Clementine Rose and the Pet Day Disaster
Clementine Rose and the Perfect Present
Clementine Rose and the Farm Fiasco

Alice-Miranda at School
Alice-Miranda on Holiday
Alice-Miranda Takes the Lead
Alice-Miranda at Sea
Alice-Miranda in New York
Alice-Miranda Shows the Way
Alice-Miranda in Paris
Alice-Miranda Shines Bright

CLEMENTINE ROSE

and the Pet Day Disaster

Jacqueline Harvey

RANDOM HOUSE AUSTRALIA

A Random House book
Published by Random House Australia Pty Ltd
Level 3, 100 Pacific Highway, North Sydney NSW 2060
www.randomhouse.com.au

First published by Random House Australia in 2013

Addresses for companies within the Random House Group can be found at
www.randomhouse.com.au/offices.

National Library of Australia
Cataloguing-in-Publication Entry

Author: Harvey, Jacqueline
Title: Clementine Rose and the pet day disaster / Jacqueline Harvey
ISBN: 978 1 74275 543 4 (pbk.)
Series: Harvey, Jacqueline. Clementine Rose; 2
Target audience: For primary school age
Subjects: Girls – Juvenile fiction
Dewey number: A823.4

Cover and internal illustrations by J.Yi
Cover design by Leanne Beattie
Internal design by Midland Typesetters
Typeset in ITC Century 12.5/19 by Midland Typesetters, Australia
Printed in Australia by Griffin Press, an accredited ISO AS/NZS
14001:2004 Environmental Management System printer

Random House Australia uses papers that are natural, renewable and
recyclable products and made from wood grown in sustainable forests.
The logging and manufacturing processes are expected to conform to the
environmental regulations of the country of origin.

For Ian, as always, and for Eden,
who looks a lot like Clementine Rose!

FIRST DAY

Clementine Rose pushed back the bed covers and slipped down onto the cool wooden floor. A full moon hung low in the sky, lighting up pockets of the garden outside and casting a yellow glow over her room. Somewhere, a shutter was banging in the breeze, keeping time like a drummer in a marching band. But that's not what woke Clementine up. She was used to the noises of Penberthy House. It talked to her all the time.

Clementine tiptoed to the end of her bed and knelt down. She rested her head on Lavender's tummy but the little pig was fast asleep in her basket. Her shallow breaths were interrupted every now and then by a snorty grunt.

'I'd better get dressed,' Clementine whispered. 'I don't want to be late on the first day.'

Clementine skipped over to her wardrobe. Hanging on the door was her favourite new outfit. There was a pretty pink and white checked tunic, white socks and red shoes. Clementine especially adored the red blazer with swirly letters embroidered on the pocket. It was her new school uniform, which she had insisted on wearing around the house for the past week. Clementine had packed and repacked her schoolbag for almost a month too.

Clementine wriggled out of her pyjamas and got dressed, buckling her shoes last of all. She brushed her hair and pinned it off her face with a red bow. She smiled at her reflection in the mirror.

'Very smart,' she whispered to herself, just as Mrs Mogg had done when Clementine had appeared at the village store in her uniform the day before. Clementine glanced at her pet, who hadn't moved a muscle. She decided to let Lavender sleep in and headed downstairs to find her mother and Uncle Digby.

On the way, she stopped to chat with her grandparents. Well, with the portraits of her grandparents that hung on the wall.

'Good morning, Granny and Grandpa. Today's that big day I was telling you all about yesterday and the day before and the day before that. I can't wait. I'll get to play with Sophie and Poppy and I'm going to learn how to read and do numbers and tell the time. Did you like school?' She peered up at her grandfather. She could have sworn he nodded his head ever so slightly.

'What about you, Granny?' She looked at the portrait of her grandmother dressed in a splendid gown, with the Appleby diamond tiara on her head. She wore the matching necklace and earrings too. Everyone had thought the jewellery was lost until Aunt Violet had found it when she came to stay. Now the tiara and earrings were safely hidden away in the vault while her mother decided what to do with them; the necklace was still missing. Uncle Digby said that if the jewellery was sold it would bring enough money to pay for a new roof, which Penberthy House badly needed. But Lady Clarissa said that she would wait a while to decide. The roof had leaked for years and they were used to putting the buckets out, so there was no hurry.

Clementine studied her grandmother's expression. There was just a hint of a lovely smile. She took that to mean that she had enjoyed school too.

Clementine looked at the next portrait along, which showed a beautiful young woman. Clementine had called her Grace until, to her surprise, her Great-Aunt Violet had arrived at the house a few months ago and revealed that she was the woman in the painting. Clementine was shocked to learn that the woman was still alive because everyone else in the pictures was long gone.

Aunt Violet and Clementine hadn't exactly hit it off when they first met but for now the old woman was away on a world cruise, so Clementine didn't have to worry about her. Sooner or later, though, she'd be back.

Uncle Digby always said that a day at the seaside would cheer anyone up. So Clementine thought Aunt Violet should be the happiest person on earth by the time she returned from her cruise. When she had told her mother and Uncle Digby that, they had both laughed and said that they hoped very much that she was right.

Downstairs in the hallway, the ancient grandfather clock began to chime. Clemmie always thought it sounded sad.

She counted the chimes out loud. 'One, two, three, four. Mummy will have to get that silly clock fixed. It can't be four o'clock because everyone knows that's in the afternoon. Have a good day,' she said to her relatives on the wall. 'I'll tell you all about school when I get home and maybe, Grandpa, I'll have learned a new poem for you.' Ever since Clemmie could talk, Uncle Digby had taught her poems, which she loved to recite. She often performed for guests who came to stay too, and even though she couldn't yet read, she had a wonderful memory.

Clementine bounced down the stairs and along the hallway to the kitchen. It was still in darkness. Pharaoh, Aunt Violet's sphynx cat, was asleep in his basket beside the stove.

'Mummy and Uncle Digby must be having a sleep-in, like Lavender and Pharaoh,' Clementine said to herself. She hoped they would be up soon.

The little girl climbed onto the stool in the pantry and pulled out a box of cereal, set a bowl and a spoon on the table and fetched the milk from the fridge.

She managed to pour her breakfast without spilling too much. Thankfully, none landed on her uniform.

Clementine listened to the sounds of the house as she ate. Sometimes when people came to stay they asked her mother if Penberthy House had any ghosts. Most children Clemmie's age would have been frightened by the idea, but she often imagined her grandfather and grandmother coming to life at night-time, stepping out of their paintings and having tea in the sitting room, or drifting through the halls.

Clementine swallowed the last spoonful of cereal. 'Good,' she said to herself. 'Now I can go as soon as Mummy and ... Uncle Digby ...' Her eyelids drooped and she yawned loudly.

She rested her head on the table and within a minute she was fast asleep.

TIME TO GO

'Clemmie.' Lady Clarissa gently stroked her daughter's hair. 'Wake up, sleepyhead.'

Clementine's face crumpled and she struggled to open her eyes until she remembered what day it was and sat bolt upright.

'Did I miss it?' she asked.

'Miss what?' her mother replied.

'School, of course.' Clementine sniffed. She could smell toast cooking.

'No, Clemmie, it's just after seven.' Her mother shook her head. 'How long have you been up?'

'I don't know. The clock chimed four times but it must be broken because that's in the afternoon,' Clementine explained.

'Oh dear, you've been up for hours, silly sausage. I hope you're not too tired for your first day.' Lady Clarissa put a plate of hot buttery toast with strawberry jam in front of her daughter. 'Four o'clock can be in the morning too, Clemmie, and it's very early – at least three hours before you usually get up.'

'Oh.' Clementine frowned. 'Well, today I'll learn how to tell the time and then I won't get up too early tomorrow.'

Digby Pertwhistle arrived in the kitchen. He had been the butler at Penberthy House for longer than anyone could remember and was more like a beloved uncle to Clarissa and Clementine than an employee. He and Clarissa ran the house as a country hotel, but unfortunately guests were few and far between.

'Good morning, Clementine. Are you all ready for the big day?' he asked, his grey eyes twinkling.

'Oh yes, Uncle Digby,' said Clementine, nodding. 'I've been ready forever.'

Digby and Clarissa smiled at one another. That was certainly true.

'Well, eat up your toast and drink your juice. You'll need lots of energy. I've packed your morning tea and I think –' her mother opened the lid of the red lunchbox which had Clementine's name written neatly on the lid – 'Uncle Digby has added a treat.' She snapped the lid closed again.

The old man winked at Clementine. She tried to wink back but she just double blinked instead.

'I've got the camera ready,' said Digby. He walked over to the sideboard and picked up a small black bag.

'Goody!' said Clementine. She finished the last bite of her toast and jumped down from the chair. 'I'll just get Lavender ready. She had a sleep-in.'

'Clemmie, I don't know if we can take her with us today,' said her mother. 'I'm not sure how the school feels about pets.'

'But I told her she could come. Please,' Clementine begged her mother.

Pharaoh let out a loud meow as he stood up in his basket and arched his back.

'No, Pharaoh, you are definitely not coming. Can you imagine what would happen if we took you to town and you got away?' Digby shook his head.

'We don't want to make Aunt Violet cross again, that's for sure,' Clementine replied. 'But Lavender will be so sad if she has to stay home. She's been looking forward to school for as long as I have.'

'Well, what about if I take care of Lavender when you and your mother go into school,' Digby suggested. 'We can go for a walk around the village and I can pop into the patisserie and see Pierre.'

'And you can get a great big cream bun for your morning tea!' Clementine announced.

'Oh, I haven't had one of Pierre's cream buns for ages.' Digby's stomach gurgled at the thought of it.

'All right, now run along, Clemmie, and brush your teeth. We'll have to leave soon,' her mother instructed.

Clementine skipped up the back stairs to her room on the third floor, singing to herself on the way, 'I get to go to school today, I can't wait, hip hip hooray ...'

OLD FRIENDS, AND NEW ENEMIES

'Look, Clementine, there's Sophie and Jules,' Lady Clarissa said as Digby Pertwhistle's ancient Mini Minor trundled to a halt outside the school gates. Clementine loved the way the ironwork on the gates was woven together with fancy letters on either side, the same as on her blazer pocket.

Ellery Prep was in the centre of Highton Mill, a short drive from her home in Penberthy Floss. The limestone school buildings nestled behind a neatly trimmed hedge, and several chimney pots poked up into the sky from the slate rooftops. Behind the classrooms and the office there was a large field where the children played at break times. The far end of the ground was bordered by an ancient stone cottage with a rambling garden of creepers and flowers that did their best to invade the school grounds.

'And there's Poppy and Jasper and Lily too!' Clementine leaned forward, craning her neck to see who else was among the group arriving at the gate.

'So, young lady, what do you think you're going to learn today?' Digby asked.

'Everything!' she exclaimed.

'Clemmie, I don't know if you'll learn *everything* on the first day,' Lady Clarissa said. 'You might have to be a little bit patient.'

'But I don't like being patient.' Clementine frowned and shook her head. Lavender grunted as if to agree.

'Oh dear, even the pig knows that's true,' Digby laughed.

'Come on, we'd better get you inside,' said Lady Clarissa as she got out of the car. Clementine hopped out and lifted Lavender off the seat and put her on the ground. Today the little pig was in her best red collar and matching lead.

Digby retrieved Clemmie's enormous backpack from the boot. 'Ready?' he asked.

'Yes. Mummy, can you take Lavender's lead for a minute?'

Digby settled the bag onto Clementine's shoulders. 'You still look like a tortoise, my dear,' he said with a smile, 'but at least now you're part of a family of tortoises.' He gestured towards the growing crowd of new students, whose gigantic bags were almost tipping them backwards.

'Clementine!' Poppy caught sight of her friend and raced towards her. Sophie saw her and rushed over too.

The three girls linked arms and giggled.

Lady Clarissa said hello to Poppy and Sophie and walked over to where their mothers, Lily

and Odette, were standing together talking. Sophie's brother Jules and Poppy's brother Jasper had disappeared inside the school grounds. They were older and knew exactly what to do.

Clementine and her friends were chatting about this and that when Clemmie noticed a boy with wild brown curls. He was standing beside a stout woman with the same brown curls and he was staring at Clementine and frowning.

She waved at him but he didn't wave back. He just kept on staring.

'Who's that boy over there?' Clementine asked her friends.

'Where?' they replied.

'Over there next to the lady with the curly hair. He keeps looking at me.'

'I don't know. I've never seen him before,' Sophie replied.

Poppy shrugged.

It was almost a quarter past nine. All the older students had disappeared into their classrooms and it was time for the new students to meet with Miss Critchley, the head teacher.

Clementine Rose thought that Miss Critchley, a pretty young woman with long auburn curls, was the most beautiful lady she'd ever seen. On the day Clemmie had gone for her interview, Miss Critchley had been wearing a pale pink cardigan with silk roses embroidered around the collar and a pale pink dress with a matching pair of ballet flats. Clementine had decided to ask Mrs Mogg if she could make her a dress just like it.

'Clementine, we have to go in,' her mother called. Lily and Odette beckoned for Poppy and Sophie to join them too.

Clementine nodded at her mother. 'I'll just say goodbye to Uncle Digby and Lavender.' She raced away to where Digby Pertwhistle was standing a little further along the footpath. Lavender had been chomping on a clump of sweet clover growing beside the fence.

'Have a wonderful day, my dear,' said Digby. He leaned down and Clementine wrapped her arms around him and kissed his cheek.

'Thank you, Uncle Digby,' she said, smiling excitedly. Then Clemmie bent down and gave Lavender a kiss on the top of her bristly head. 'Be a good girl for Uncle Digby and I will see you after school.'

Lavender grunted.

'No, you can't come with me, Lavender. Mummy says there's a rule that pigs aren't allowed to go to school.' Clementine sighed. 'I know, it's silly, but I shouldn't break the rules on my first day.' Clemmie then leaned down and whispered into Lavender's ear. 'One day, I'll find a way for you to come.'

'Run along, Clemmie, you don't want to be late. I think I'll go and pay Pierre that visit.' Digby winked at the girl.

Clementine double blinked back at him. She hadn't noticed that the boy with curly hair was still staring at her.

As Digby strolled off, the boy approached Clementine. 'Your dad's a hundred,' he said.

Clementine looked at him and frowned. 'My dad? Oh, you mean Uncle Digby. He's not

21

my dad,' she replied. 'And he's not a hundred. He's seventy-one.'

'Where's your dad, then?' the boy asked.

'He's a mystery,' Clementine replied.

'He's a mystery?' the boy repeated. 'That's stupid. How can a dad be a mystery?'

'I don't know exactly, but mine is,' Clementine replied. She'd never been asked about her father before. Everyone in Penberthy Floss knew that she had arrived at Lady Clarissa's house in the back of Pierre Rousseau's van, in a basket of dinner rolls. It had been an unusual way to join a family, but the adoption papers had all been in order and Clementine had definitely gone to the right home.

Clementine wanted to tell the boy that he was stupid too but then she remembered what her mother and Uncle Digby were always telling her: 'If you can't say something nice, don't say anything at all.'

She kept quiet and rushed off to her mother, except that her tongue poked out at him at the last second. She didn't really mean to. It just sort of happened. ·

'Well, excuse me, young lady!' The boy's curly-haired mother had reappeared just in time to spot Clemmie's lizard tongue. 'You're a rude little creature, aren't you?'

Clementine felt like a thousand butterflies were having a party in her tummy. And they hadn't been invited.

A NEW
TEACHER

The children and their parents were ushered into the small school hall, which also doubled as the gymnasium. Clementine sat next to her mother with Sophie on the other side and Poppy along further. There were twenty children starting in the kindergarten class. Miss Critchley approached the microphone and welcomed the students and their parents.

Clementine was busy studying the young woman's outfit. Today she had on a dark blue blouse with a bow at the front and a pair of grey pants. Her hair was pulled back softly from her face. Clementine still thought she was the most beautiful lady she'd ever seen.

'Now, I know that some of you might be sitting there with a few butterflies in your tummy,' said Miss Critchley with a kind smile at the group. 'But let me assure you, that's absolutely normal. I imagine you're a little bit nervous and a little bit excited all in one.'

Clementine nodded. So did lots of the other children. Miss Critchley definitely knew a lot about kindergartners, Clementine thought to herself.

'I just need to go through some of the school procedures so that we all know what we're doing and then I will introduce you to your class teacher.'

Clementine wondered if she'd misheard her. Wasn't Miss Critchley going to be their teacher? She didn't want to have anyone else.

'In the afternoon, all of the students will wait for their parents at the school gate under the supervision of a teacher, unless of course you live here in the village. If so, you can walk home and perhaps in the future you might like to ride your bike to and from school ...'

Clementine wasn't listening. She was wondering who was going to be their teacher. The butterflies in her tummy now seemed to be having a boxing match. She didn't like this one bit.

'We encourage parents to come along and help with reading and other activities in the classroom ...'

Clementine's eyes darted around the room, looking for the person who could be their teacher. There was a man in the front row. He had greasy hair and the tail of a dragon tattoo poking out from his shirt sleeve. But then she saw a little girl sitting beside him and guessed he was one of the fathers. There was a lady with blonde hair at the far end. Perhaps it was her.

'And now I'd like to introduce Mrs Ethel Bottomley, who'll be teaching the kindergarten class this year. Mrs Bottomley has many years of experience and is an excellent educator. I know she's looking forward to working with you all.'

Clementine's stomach lurched as she looked up and saw a short woman wearing a drab brown check jacket and matching skirt heading for the microphone. Mrs Bottomley's low-heeled brown shoes clacked on the timber floor and were just about the ugliest things Clementine had ever seen. A helmet of brown curls perched on top of her head and Clementine thought they reminded her of someone else.

'Good morning, parents and children, my name is Ethel Bottomley.' She spoke with a very strange voice. It was whispery but posh at the same time. 'We all know that kindergarten is a very important time in every child's life. It's a time to shake off the playful habits of youth and start some serious study. Rest assured there will be time for fun – orderly fun, of course. And parents, please know that I have high standards and very high expectations. The children will

not be spoiled under my care.' The old woman grinned, revealing a row of yellowed teeth.

Clementine recoiled in her seat.

'But I don't want her,' she whispered to her mother.

'Clementine, I'm sure that Mrs Bottomley is perfectly lovely. You just need to get to know her,' her mother whispered back. But Clarissa felt a little uncertain too. Mrs Bottomley wasn't quite what she had in mind when she pictured her daughter's kindergarten teacher either.

Miss Critchley returned to the microphone. 'Thank you, Mrs Bottomley. Now we should be getting to class, children. Please say goodbye to your parents and follow Mrs Bottomley to the door.'

Clementine felt as if there was a wedge of bread stuck in her throat.

'Goodbye, Clemmie, have a lovely day,' said Clarissa, as she blinked back a tear. She'd been determined not to cry but she hadn't imagined how hard it would be to see her baby starting school.

Clementine clung to her mother. She didn't want to let go.

Sophie reached for her hand. 'Come on.'

'No.' Clementine felt the sting of tears prickling her eyes.

'Clemmie, it's all right,' her friend Poppy tried.

'You have to go, sweetheart. It will be lots of fun,' her mother said. She tried to prise loose Clemmie's arms, which were clamped firmly around her middle.

Arabella Critchley noticed her reluctant student and approached the group.

'Hello Clementine, it's lovely to see you.' She crouched down to meet the child's gaze. Clementine's blue eyes looked like pools of wet ink. 'Do you want to come with me?'

Clementine shook her head.

'I don't know what's got into her,' whispered Lady Clarissa as Miss Critchley stood up. 'She's been looking forward to school for weeks. It's been a battle to get her to wear anything other than her uniform.'

The rest of the class was now standing at the door in two higgledy-piggledy lines.

'Kindergarten, let's see if we can straighten up. Now!' Mrs Bottomley barked.

The children snapped to attention and the lines became perfectly parallel under her outstretched arms.

'Clementine, why don't I take you to class?' Miss Critchley tried again.

Clementine didn't know why she was holding onto her mother. She'd been so excited about school and now Sophie and Poppy were going to start without her.

'Is that little one going to join us?' Mrs Bottomley called from the front of the line. 'Or is she having a bit of a sook?'

'We'll be along in a minute,' Miss Critchley replied firmly. She brushed a rogue strand of hair away from Clementine's face.

Clementine felt silly. She wanted to go with the rest of her class. She didn't want to be last and she didn't want to be called a sook.

'You know, Clementine, on my first day of

school I didn't want to go either. My older brother had told me all sorts of terrible stories and I was scared stiff,' Miss Critchley explained.

'What stories?' Clementine whispered.

'He told me that the headmaster had a secret cupboard full of canes and that he walked around the school whacking children willy-nilly,' said Miss Critchley. 'And you know what? None of it was true. He'd only said it to make me afraid and he succeeded. Is there anything you're afraid of?'

'I thought you were going to be my teacher,' Clementine said, frowning. 'I don't want Mrs Bottom.'

'You mean Mrs Bottomley, Clementine, and I can assure you that her bark is much worse than her bite. She comes across as being a bit stern but she's a big squishy marshmallow underneath,' Miss Critchley explained.

'A big squishy *brown* marshmallow,' Clementine whispered.

'What do you mean?' Miss Critchley asked.

'It must be her favourite colour,' Clementine said.

'Oh,' Miss Critchley smiled. She realised that Clementine was referring to Mrs Bottomley's clothes. 'That's right, you were quite the stylish young lady when you came for your interview and you asked me about my dress.'

Clementine's eyes sparkled and she seemed to perk up.

'Shall we go to class?' The head teacher asked. Clementine released her mother from the vice-like grip and put her hand into Miss Critchley's. They headed for the door.

Suddenly Clemmie ran back and gave Lady Clarissa a final hug. 'Bye Mummy!'

'See you this afternoon, Clemmie, and have a wonderful day,' Lady Clarissa sniffed.

Clementine Rose arrived at her classroom just as Mrs Bottomley was calling the roll and asking the children to stand in alphabetical order at the back of the room.

Poppy was standing beside the curly-haired boy Clementine had seen outside the school.

'Excuse me, Mrs Bottomley,' Miss Critchley interrupted. 'This is Clementine Rose Appleby.'

'Hello dear. You've got over the wobbles, I see. Very good. Appleby. You're first on the

34

roll so you'll need to stand next to Angus up the back there. Angus, put up your hand so Clementine knows who you are.'

The boy with the curly hair raised his hand slightly. Clementine wondered why they had to line up again inside the classroom. There was a lot of time-wasting at school, she decided.

Reluctantly, Clementine walked to the back of the room and stood beside the boy.

Poppy stood on his other side. She leaned around him and asked, 'Are you all right?'

Clementine nodded. She didn't want to talk about what had happened earlier. It made her feel all red.

Mrs Bottomley continued calling names until everyone was standing at the back of the room.

'I have just placed you in what we call alphabetical order. Can anyone tell me what that is?'

A sharp-looking girl with a face like a fieldmouse shot her hand into the air.

'Yes, Astrid,' Mrs Bottomley called.

'It's when you put words into order using the letter of the alphabet that they start with,' the child replied.

'Very good. Now, can anyone tell me if I've put you into alphabetical order according to your first names or surnames?'

Clementine wondered what she was talking about. So did the rest of the class, except for the mouse child who put her hand up again.

'Yes, Astrid.'

'That's easy. It's our surnames, because if it was our first names I'd be standing up there near Angus and Anna but she's at the end of the line because her last name starts with a "W".'

'Goodness me, what a clever little girl you are.' Mrs Bottomley beamed at Astrid. Clementine had no idea what Mrs Bottomley was talking about but she wished she would hurry up and teach her how to read. Surely that would take up most of the day.

'I'd like you to sit next to your partner. Angus, you're sitting with Clementine.' The old woman ushered the pair to the front of the room, where she instructed them to sit down at the first double desk. All of the desks formed neat pairs in neat rows. Clementine wondered if Mrs Bottomley had a thing about lines.

'But I don't want to sit with her,' Angus said and pulled a face.

'Angus Archibald, you'll do exactly as you're told, young man.' The teacher glared at the lad.

Clementine almost felt sorry for him. Just for a moment.

Angus slid into his seat and slumped down, resting his elbows on the desk.

'Was that a pig outside with the old guy?' he mumbled.

'Yes,' Clementine replied quietly.

'Is it *your* pig?' The boy turned and looked at her with his head lying on the desk.

Clementine nodded.

'Where does it live?' he asked.

Clementine started to soften. 'She sleeps in a basket at the end of my bed.'

'Pooh!' the boy scoffed. 'That's so dumb. A smelly pig in your bedroom!'

Clementine couldn't help herself. 'Lavender's not smelly at all. She's smart and she's clean and I love her,' she said sharply.

'You love a pig.' Angus turned around to the boy who was sitting behind them. 'She loves a pig.' He pointed at Clementine and oinked.

Clementine felt hot. The collar of her blazer was prickling her skin and she wanted him to stop.

Angus screwed up his face. 'A stupid pig won't win the pet competition.'

'What pet competition?' Clementine asked.

'It's a secret,' Angus bragged. 'I know all the secrets around here and no smelly pigs will be allowed because Miss Critchley hates them.'

Clementine decided to ignore him but she wondered if it was true. Surely Miss Critchley didn't hate pigs, especially not Lavender. She didn't even know her yet.

Mrs Bottomley appeared at the front of the room. She had a marker pen in her hand and was waving it wildly in the air. 'Now that everyone finally has a seat, it's time that we got on with some work.' She approached the whiteboard and wrote the letter 'A', which Clementine recognised. Her last name started with an 'A'. Finally she was going to learn how to read.

'Now this, my little empty vessels, is where we will begin. Can anyone tell me something they can see in the classroom beginning with "A"?'

Astrid's arm shot up like a spring.

'Yes, Astrid,' the teacher beamed.

'Astrid starts with an "A",' she replied, 'and there's an apple on your desk.'

'So there is.' Mrs Bottomley nodded and wrote two words on the board. 'Yes, what were you going to say, Angus?'

'Angus starts with "A" and so does her name,' he pointed at Clementine. 'Applebum.' The boy burst out laughing. Some of the other children giggled, except for a boy at the back of the room who clucked like a chicken.

Clementine glared at Angus.

'Angus Archibald, you need to find some manners, young man, or you'll be out the door and over to see Miss Critchley,' Mrs Bottomley threatened. 'And as for the rest of you,' she said with a glare that silenced the class, 'settle down immediately.'

The lesson continued until the whiteboard was covered in words, none of which Clementine could read at all. She wondered when the lessons would start properly.

The morning dragged on. They did some colouring in and traced the outlines of words with pencils. Clementine tried hard to stay in the lines but it wasn't as easy as she'd thought it would be. And then when she walked over to sharpen a pencil someone scribbled all over the bottom of her page.

'Did you do that?' she asked Angus as she sat back down.

He shook his head. 'No.'

Clementine got up and walked over to Mrs Bottomley's desk, where the teacher was busy thumbing through a magazine.

'Excuse me, Mrs Bottomley. May I please have a new sheet because someone drew all over the bottom of this one?' Clementine asked.

The teacher looked up and sighed.

'I don't have any spare sheets. And I'm sure that no one *else* drew on the page, did they, Clementine? You just have to learn to be more careful with your work.'

'But Angus did it,' Clementine protested.

'Angus,' Mrs Bottomley called across the room. 'Did you make this mess all over Clementine's work?'

'No,' the boy replied, shaking his head slowly. He blinked innocently.

'All right, thank you.' She turned her attention back to Clementine. 'Now, I know that Angus made a silly comment earlier but he's really a very good boy and I can't imagine that he'd be lying about the worksheet. It's very important, Clementine, now that you're a big girl at school, to always tell the truth. And it's really not nice to be a dibber-dobber, you know.'

'But I am telling the truth,' Clementine retorted.

Mrs Bottomley was not going to back down

any more than Clementine was. 'Did you see Angus draw on your sheet?'

'No, but he did it,' Clementine asserted.

'There is no proof, Clementine, so you'll just have to make the best of it and paste that one into your book the way I showed you. It's a pity that your first piece of work is rather messy but I suppose that's a good lesson to learn about doing your best.'

Clementine felt hot and prickly again.

'When are we going to learn to read?' Clementine asked.

'You've been learning that all morning,' Mrs Bottomley smiled.

'Oh.' Clementine frowned and took her sheet back to her desk. She sat down and opened her workbook and pasted the paper into the front. It looked awful.

Angus leaned over and whispered, 'Guess what? I did it.'

Clementine was shocked. 'Mrs Bottomley, Angus just told me that he scribbled on my page,' she called out.

'Did not,' Angus sneered at her.

'Clementine, you really must stop all these false accusations at once,' Mrs Bottomley huffed. 'You don't want to get a reputation for telling tales on your very first day, do you?'

Clementine finished pasting her page into the book and snapped it shut. She looked at the clock and hoped that it would soon be time for morning tea.

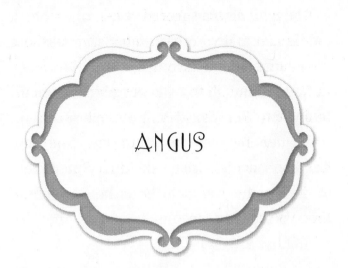

ANGUS

Morning tea time came and went in a blink. Clementine sat with Sophie and Poppy out on the veranda and by the time the girls had eaten their snacks and visited the toilet there was no time left to play.

Clementine had decided that visiting the toilet was very important. Just before the morning tea bell, a girl called Erica had an accident in the classroom. Although Mrs Bottomley didn't fuss, Erica cried and everyone felt sorry for her. That is, except for some of the boys, including Angus, who called her a piddle-pants. Mrs Bottomley told the class that it could happen to anyone.

Clementine didn't like to think it could happen to her. She'd had enough attention from her teacher for one day. She had already decided that she'd try her best to do as she was told and then hopefully Mrs Bottomley wouldn't accuse her of telling lies any more.

After morning tea, Mrs Bottomley made the children copy some numbers from the board and then match them with coloured blocks. Clementine wondered when she would learn how to tell the time.

She avoided talking to Angus and tried not to look at him either. But that didn't stop him being naughty.

Clementine just happened to glance up from her work when she saw that Angus was drilling his finger up his nose. She watched as he removed a large glob of yellow snot. He held it in the air and examined it closely.

Angus noticed her watching him and pulled a face. 'What are you looking at?'

'Nothing,' said Clementine, and went back to her work. That's when Angus did something unforgivable. He wiped his finger on her shoulder.

She let out a squeal. 'Ahh!'

'Clementine Rose Appleby, whatever is the matter now?' Mrs Bottomley demanded.

'Angus just put snot on my uniform.' Clementine's lip began to tremble. Her beautiful clean new uniform now had a disgusting booger on it.

'Come here,' said Mrs Bottomley, rolling her eyes.

Clementine stood up. Angus giggled. The boy behind him called Joshua laughed too.

But this time the girls in the class seemed equally offended and nine pairs of eyes bored into Angus's back.

Mrs Bottomley examined the offending yellow glob. With one swift move she pulled a tissue from the supersized box on her desk

and removed it without so much as leaving a mark.

'All gone, Clementine, nothing to worry about,' she tutted. 'Angus Archibald, you will see me at lunchtime. I think our playground could do with some beautification, which you will be in charge of. That behaviour is completely unacceptable.' The teacher walked over to the lad, who crossed his arms and huffed loudly.

'But,' he whined, 'it was an accident.'

Mrs Bottomley's eyebrows furrowed together like a pair of angry brown caterpillars. 'I don't think so.'

'But, Nan . . .' Angus pouted.

The whole class gasped.

'What did you just call me?' Ethel Bottomley's eyes grew round and she stood over him like a giant brown toadstool.

Clementine looked at Angus Archibald and then at Mrs Bottomley. They had the same hair; that was why she had thought Mrs Bottomley reminded her of someone. It was the woman who had been standing out the front with Angus. She must be Mrs Bottomley's daughter.

Angus looked at the forbidding woman in front of him.

'Outside. NOW!' she roared.

The lad scurried out the door and onto the veranda like a naughty dog. The kindergarten class had never been left on their own before. No one quite knew what to do.

Sophie and Poppy left their seats and raced up the front to talk to Clementine.

'He's in big trouble now,' Sophie said.

'But if Mrs Bottomley's really his granny, she can't be all that mad with him. Grandparents have to be nice to their grandchildren,' said Poppy. 'It's in the rules.'

'Are you joking? My grandmamma is fierce and French and half the time I can't understand a word she says. She scares me to bits,' Sophie said.

It was hard to tell what was going on out on the veranda, except when Mrs Bottomley roared like a hungry lion.

'It doesn't sound like he's getting any special treatment,' said Clementine. Her eyes were the size of dinner plates.

'Don't you ever call me Nan in class again, young man, or I will have you out of here before you have time to learn to count to one hundred,' Mrs Bottomley bellowed.

The door opened and everyone scurried back to their seats, like ants before a storm.

'Yes, well,' the teacher said, looking around at the class, 'we might as well be honest about this. Angus is my grandson. But rest assured, while I love him very much, he will call me Mrs Bottomley just the same as everyone else does.' She glared at the lad, whose face was red and eyes were puffy. He sniffled as he skulked back to his desk.

Clementine thought that was a bit beside the point. Who cared if he called her Nan? She was more worried about him getting away with bad behaviour, which up until now he'd proven to be very good at. Angus slumped down in his chair. He wiped his eyes with the back of his hands.

Clementine felt a little bit sorry for him. She decided to see if he would talk to her. Maybe then he wouldn't be so upset.

'Are we really having a pet day?' Clementine asked.

Angus shrugged.

Clementine tried again to be friendly. 'That would be fun, don't you think?'

'Maybe,' Angus said with a sniffle.

Clementine noticed that he was in need of a tissue. She walked over to Mrs Bottomley's supersized box, pulled a couple out and handed them to the boy. He took the tissues from her and blew his nose like a trumpet, then thrust them back at her covered in gooey slime.

'You just don't get it, do you?' Clementine sighed, and then dropped the grotty tissues in the bin. She asked Mrs Bottomley if she could go to the toilet and wash her hands. Angus hadn't even said thank you.

LUNCHTIME

Clementine's tummy grumbled and she was very glad when Mrs Bottomley announced that it was time for lunch. The teacher had the children stand in two straight lines and marched them across the quadrangle. Clementine was quite sure now that Mrs Bottomley had a thing about lines.

Because the kindergarten children took longer to eat their lunch, they arrived at the dining room a quarter of an hour before the other classes. That way they had a better chance of finishing their meal and still having time for a run around in the playground before the afternoon lessons.

'Lunch today is Mrs Winky's special sausages with yummy mashed potato and vegetables,' Mrs Bottomley told the group.

Clementine thought that sounded quite good – she loved her mother's sausages and mashed potato. The children lined up once again and the plates of food were handed over to them.

'It smells nice,' Poppy said as she walked over to a table and sat down.

'No, no, no, Poppy, you must sit where I tell you to,' Mrs Bottomley barked. 'Over there with Clementine and Angus and Joshua. I think it's far better to have the girls and boys mixed together at lunchtime.'

Clementine couldn't believe that she had to sit with Angus again.

She put her plate down on the table and realised that she needed to go to the toilet. She didn't want to leave it until later, just in case she had an accident too.

She whispered to Poppy.

'I need to go too,' Poppy replied.

The girls approached Mrs Bottomley and asked if they could go. The old woman huffed and asked why they hadn't gone at morning tea time.

'But we did,' Clementine protested.

Mrs Bottomley muttered something that sounded like 'weak bladders' and then said, 'I'm not too keen to mop up after anyone else today, so yes, off you go.'

The girls returned just minutes later. Angus and Joshua were sitting at the table grinning at one another like a pair of Cheshire cats.

'What are you smiling at?' Clementine asked as she sat down.

'Nothing.' Angus shook his head.

'Yeah, nothing at all,' Joshua added, which only made Clementine more suspicious.

Clementine pushed her fork into the mashed potato and put it in her mouth.

Poppy did the same.

At exactly the same moment both girls spat their mouthfuls of food all over their plates.

'Yuck!' Clementine couldn't get it out quickly enough. 'That's disgusting!'

Poppy was gagging.

Mrs Bottomley was patrolling the tables and saw their carry-on. 'Girls, whatever's the matter this time?'

'There's something wrong with it,' said Clementine. She pointed at the potato. 'It tastes awful.'

'I'll be the judge of that.' Mrs Bottomley whisked the fork out of Angus's hand and dug it into his mashed potato. She shovelled a generous portion of the creamy white vegetable into her mouth.

'Mmm, delicious,' she said. She looked at Clementine and Poppy. 'There's nothing wrong with this at all.'

'I'm sure there's nothing wrong with *Angus's* food because he wouldn't do anything to his own lunch,' Clementine snapped.

'Are you accusing Angus of tampering with

your food?' Mrs Bottomley stared at her. Even her eyebrows looked sharp.

'He must have put something in it when Poppy and me went to the toilet,' said Clementine. She could feel the hot sting of tears prickling her eyes for the second time that day. She also noticed some sprinklings of what looked like salt all over the floor.

'That would be "Poppy and I", Clementine.' The teacher turned to her grandson. 'Angus, did you put anything in the girls' lunch?'

'No, Na– … I mean, Mrs Bottomley. I didn't and he didn't either.' Angus pointed at Joshua, who covered his mouth.

'But he's smiling,' Poppy said.

'Don't tell me you're going to get in on this act as well, Miss Bauer? My patience is just about worn through today,' the teacher snarled.

Poppy looked as if she might cry too.

'I saw a lovely chocolate pudding for dessert but that's only for the children who eat up everything on their plates,' said Mrs Bottomley. 'You'd better tuck in, hadn't you?'

She turned to walk away and Poppy pulled a face at her. It wasn't fair.

'What is it?' Clementine demanded, glaring at Angus.

He smiled sweetly. 'What do you mean?'

'What did you put on there?' she asked again.

'I told you, we didn't put anything on it.'

'You're lying.' Clementine wanted to go home. She'd had more than enough school for one day.

Angus and his partner in crime finished their meals and took their plates back to the servery.

'He's horrible,' Poppy said, pushing the salty potato about on her plate.

'They're both horrible,' Clementine said.

The two lads returned to the table with giant servings of chocolate pudding and ice-cream.

'Mmm, yum, this is so sweet,' Angus said with his mouth full. 'Not salty at all.' He smiled at Joshua, who grinned back.

'Yeah, sweet,' Joshua replied, giggling.

Clementine glared at the two boys. She wanted some too.

'Come on, Poppy, bring your plate.' She picked hers up and walked towards the servery.

'But Mrs Bottomley said that we could only have it if we ate all our dinner.' Poppy looked sadly at the two plates that were still full of food.

Clementine was watching as the children at the end of the line put their dinner scraps in the bin. Mrs Bottomley was supervising the drink station, where one of the girls had flicked on the tap to the cordial container and couldn't work out how to turn it off. There was a flood of raspberry crush pooling on the floor and Mrs Bottomley was shrieking for someone to get a towel.

With their teacher and Mrs Winky busy cleaning up, Clementine scraped her plate into the bin, then did the same with Poppy's. She placed the empty plates on the servery and picked up a chocolate pudding for herself and another for Poppy.

'But Mrs Bottomley said we had to eat it all,' Poppy said.

'Mrs Bottomley's not fair,' Clementine replied. 'And I'm hungry.'

Poppy nodded. She was hungry too. The girls headed back to the table, where Angus and Joshua were now showering each other with sprinklings of salt and sugar.

'You didn't eat your lunch,' Angus said. 'I'm telling Nan on you.'

'And I'll tell Mrs Bottomley that you called her Nan again,' Clementine threatened. 'And that you put salt all over our lunch.'

'Yeah, we did,' Joshua admitted, grinning.

Angus elbowed Joshua. 'She loves pigs.'

She narrowed her eyes at him. 'Yes, I do love my pig.'

'*You're* a pig,' Joshua said.

Clementine didn't like being called names. She'd never met anyone like Angus or Joshua and she didn't like the way they made her feel one little bit.

NOT GOING

'My tummy hurts.' Clementine lay in bed clutching her stomach. Tears sprouted from her eyes and rolled down her cheeks.

'Oh, sweetheart.' Her mother sat down beside her. 'You poor little floss. I can't believe that you're sick and it's only the second day of school.'

Clarissa laid the back of her hand on Clementine's forehead. She didn't seem to have a fever.

But something certainly wasn't right. When Clarissa had met Clementine at the school gate yesterday afternoon she had expected her to be fizzing like a shaken bottle of lemonade, but instead she was flatter than a week-old glass of cola. When she had asked about her day, Clementine said that it was okay. Clarissa was worried. It was as if the child she'd delivered to school that morning had been exchanged for another that she barely recognised at all.

'So what was Mrs Bottomley really like?' Lady Clarissa had asked as they scooted along in the car on their way home.

'Brown,' Clementine had replied.

'Clemmie, there must be more to her than that,' her mother had said. 'Did you have fun with Sophie and Poppy?'

Clementine had nodded but her mouth stayed closed.

'Are you feeling all right?'

Clementine had shaken her head. Fat tears had wobbled in the corners of her eyes and rolled down her cheeks. Lady Clarissa had

watched in the rear-view mirror as Clementine wiped them away.

That night Clementine had picked at her dinner, which was most unusual given that it was her favourite: roast lamb with baked potatoes, beans and gravy.

When Clarissa went to check on Clementine later, she found her sound asleep. Her uniform was strewn all over the floor, not hanging proudly on the wardrobe door as it had been for weeks.

Now Lavender was sitting guard on the floor in a bright patch of morning light and Pharaoh was snuggled in beside Clementine on the bed. Lavender looked as worried as Lady Clarissa felt.

Digby Pertwhistle appeared at Clementine's bedroom door. He knocked gently before entering, carrying a tea tray with two boiled eggs and toasty soldiers.

'Good morning, Clementine. Your mother tells me you're not feeling well,' he said with a frown.

'Do I have to go to school?' Clementine asked between teary hiccups.

Clarissa couldn't remember ever seeing Clementine cry as much. Not even when she was a baby. 'If you're not well, Clementine, I think we'll take you over to see Dr Everingham,' she said. 'Should we do that?'

Clementine nodded.

'I'll call the surgery and make you an appointment.' Digby put the tea tray down on Clementine's desk. 'Oh, and in other good news, Aunt Violet called this morning. She'll be back from her cruise this afternoon and has demanded that I pick her up from the dock.'

Digby grimaced and Clementine pinched her lips together trying not to smile.

He raised his eyebrows. 'It'll be lovely to have the demanding old dragon back again, won't it?'

Clarissa rolled her eyes and shook her head. 'Just what we need. At least this weekend there aren't any guests booked in. I think it would be best if we had some time with just the four of us, to get used to how things will work.'

'How long will Aunt Violet stay?' Clementine asked.

'I suspect she could be with us forever,' said Clarissa. 'She has nowhere else to go. She's not the easiest person to get along with but she is your grandfather's sister and I can't just throw her out on the street. Your grandfather and Aunt Violet were very close once. And I remember that when I was a girl she was jolly good fun. I just hope we can find that Violet again.'

'Under all those barnacles,' Clementine said.

'Yes, Clemmie, underneath all her crustiness,' her mother agreed.

'But she can't have my room,' Clementine said.

'Of course she won't have your room, Clemmie,' her mother replied. 'Why would you even think that?'

'When she was here before, I found her in my room and she said that this was *her* room when she was little and she might like to have it again and make it the way it should be.' Clementine's face crumpled as she spoke.

'Oh, sweetheart, there's no chance of that happening. I'm putting my foot down this time. She's having the Blue Room along the corridor up here, whether she likes it or not,' Clarissa said firmly.

'Hear, hear,' Digby agreed. 'I'd best go and make that call to the doctor.' The old man disappeared from the room.

Lavender was snuffling about on the floor at Lady Clarissa's feet. 'Hello you, why don't you give Clemmie a cuddle and see if you can make her feel better,' the woman said. She lifted the little pig up onto the bedclothes.

Clementine hugged Lavender. Pharaoh began to purr loudly beside her too.

'I'll come and let you know when we're seeing Dr Everingham,' said Clarissa, then kissed the top of Clementine's head. She looked at Clementine's uniform, which she'd hung back up on the wardrobe door the night before. 'Clemmie, is there anything else you're not telling me? Did something happen yesterday?'

Clementine shook her head. She didn't want to talk about Angus or Mrs Bottomley or how the whole day was rubbish. She hadn't learned to read or write or do numbers and she still couldn't tell the time.

After lunch, when she and Poppy and Sophie had gone to play, Angus and Joshua had followed them and wouldn't go away. When the girls had finally agreed to a game of chasings, Angus scared Clementine half to death by hunting her into the overgrown garden at the end of the field and saying that a witch lived there. Then the school caretaker Mr Pickles had crashed into the garden and yelled that the children weren't allowed in there because it wasn't safe.

In the afternoon, Mrs Bottomley had made them all lie down on the floor. She said that she as going to read them a story but then she started flipping through the magazine on her desk and making shushing noises. She told them that they should close their eyes and have a little nap. Clementine felt like a baby. She hadn't had an afternoon nap since she was three.

She hadn't told her mother yet, but she wasn't going back to school. There was no point. She could still see Sophie and Poppy at the weekend and she'd learn more from her mother and Uncle Digby than Mrs Bottomley. On top of that she wouldn't have to worry about Angus and Joshua and all the mean things they did.

She was hoping that Dr Everingham would help her tell her mother that this was for the best.

PLAN B

Uncle Digby managed to get an appointment first thing. So, just before half past eight, Clarissa and Clementine set off to Highton Mill, where the doctor had his surgery. There was no one else waiting when they arrived.

'Good morning, Lady Appleby,' the receptionist said and then looked at Clementine. 'Hello, you must be Clementine Rose. I'm Daisy.' The pretty young woman smiled at the child. Clementine said hello but didn't smile back. 'How old are you?'

'I'm five,' Clementine replied.

'Have you started school yet?' the lady asked.

Clementine nodded. She hadn't seen this woman before. Usually Mrs Minchin sat in the big chair behind the tall desk.

'Hello, Daisy is it? It was her first day yesterday,' Lady Clarissa volunteered. 'How long have you been working here?'

'Not long. I'm just relieving while Mrs Minchin's on holidays. I usually work over at Highton Hall.'

Clementine walked towards the box of toys in the corner. She could hear her mother and the lady talking but she didn't want to listen.

Dr Everingham's door opened and a tall man with a thick head of grey hair appeared at the entrance.

'Good morning, Lady Clarissa.' He walked into the reception area and looked around. 'Hello Clementine.'

Clemmie looked up from where she was examining a rather dog-eared book.

'You'd better come through so we can see what the matter is,' the doctor said with a friendly smile.

Clementine dropped the book back in the box and stood beside Clarissa. She slipped her hand into her mother's.

Inside the doctor's office was an examination table with a small stool to climb up on, a giant desk and three chairs – one for the doctor and two for patients.

Lady Clarissa and Clementine walked in and sat down.

Dr Everingham closed the door and sat down heavily in his leather office chair. He pushed back and swivelled around to face Clementine. He looked at her intently.

'Now tell me, what seems to be the matter?'

'My tummy hurts,' Clementine replied.

'I see. Can you show me where?'

Clementine touched her stomach in the middle and then on the side and further up.

'Is anything else the matter?' he said as he studied her face for clues.

Clementine shook her head.

'And when did it start to hurt?' he asked.

'At school,' she replied.

'And you only started school yesterday, isn't that right?' he asked.

Clementine nodded.

'I'm afraid, Dr Everingham, that I hardly recognised the little girl I picked up yesterday afternoon,' said Lady Clarissa, frowning.

'Ah, I see,' said the doctor.

Clementine knew that he would understand.

'So, what was school like, Clementine?' he asked. 'Did you have a good day?'

Clementine thought about what she would say. There was a long silence.

'Dr Everingham asked you a question, sweetheart. It's polite to answer,' her mother said encouragingly.

Clementine gulped. She knew that if she told Dr Everingham, he would understand. She had known him since she was a baby – although she couldn't remember all that way back. He'd always been kind. When she had to have needles he was very gentle and always gave her a lolly at the end for being brave.

'It was terrible,' Clementine blurted. 'I hate it and I'm not going back again.' A tear started to form in the corner of Clementine's eye. She brushed it away.

'Oh dear,' the doctor replied. 'That doesn't sound good. Can you tell me what happened?'

Clementine took a deep breath. She started at the very beginning with Angus saying mean things about her father and Uncle Digby. She told him about Mrs Brown Bottomley and all that silly lining up. Then there was the scribble on the bottom of her stencil and how she hadn't learned how to read or tell the time. It was as if someone had opened a floodgate: once Clementine started she couldn't stop.

Her mother sat beside her taking it all in. Now everything made perfect sense.

'Oh dear, that's no good at all, Clementine,' the doctor said when she finally paused. 'And do you think that's why you have a tummy ache?'

Clementine nodded. 'So you need to write a letter to the school telling them that I'm not coming back and I'm going to stay at home and Mummy and Uncle Digby are going to teach me everything instead,' she said firmly.

The two adults exchanged a secret look.

'I'm afraid, Clementine, I can't do that,' the doctor said seriously. 'You have to go to school. It's the law. And besides, I'm sure that things will get better. I'll bet you'll be reading and writing in no time flat. And as for that Angus, he'll have to start behaving himself. His grandmother can't be that silly. Sooner or later he'll do something really revolting and she won't be able to ignore it.'

'But he wiped snot on my uniform!' Clementine wondered how much more revolting he could be. She couldn't believe what she was hearing. Dr Everingham could fix everything. Why wouldn't he just write a note and let her stay home forever?

'I can give you something to help your tummy settle down,' he said. 'But you know the best way to feel better is to go back to school.' He looked at his watch. 'If you hurry, you could still get there in time.'

'But I don't want to go,' Clementine said.

'What about we talk to Miss Critchley and see if she can help?' her mother suggested.

Clementine Rose now knew what that mouse Pharaoh had cornered in the kitchen last week must have felt like. Her mother was on Dr Everingham's side too.

'Clementine, I'm sure that your mother is right. Miss Critchley is a very sensible woman. I should know. She's going to marry my son later this year.' The doctor's eyes twinkled.

'Oh.' Clementine's eyes lit up. She liked the idea of Miss Critchley as a bride. 'Do you think she can really help?' Clementine asked.

'I'm sure she can,' Lady Clarissa agreed. The doctor nodded too.

'What about my uniform?' Clementine asked her mother.

'I packed it into the car just in case,' Lady Clarissa replied.

There was no getting out of it.

'Would you like a jellybean?' The doctor popped the lid off the jar and held it out to Clementine.

She looked at her mother.

'Go on, Clemmie, it might make you feel better,' her mother said.

'And how's that pig of yours?' Dr Everingham asked.

'She's good. But she'll be sad because I told her that I wasn't going back to school any more and that we could stay at home and play. And now she'll just have Pharaoh and he doesn't like playing all that much,' Clementine replied.

'Can you keep a secret, Clementine?' asked the doctor.

'What sort of a secret?' she asked.

'Miss Critchley came to dinner with Mrs Everingham and our son Markus last night and she was telling us about something very special that she's planning for the school,' the doctor explained.

'What is it?' Clementine asked.

'She's going to make the announcement to the students this afternoon,' he said. 'I can't tell you all the details but I think it has something to do with pets and a very important lady.'

'Pets? At school?' Clementine's blue eyes widened. 'So Angus really was telling the truth. He said that we were having a pet competition. But then he wouldn't tell me any more.'

'Something like that,' the doctor said. 'But you won't find out if you don't go to school.'

Surely Dr Everingham wouldn't be playing a trick on her, Clementine thought. Doctors knew everything. And Angus probably knew too because Mrs Bottomley was his granny and she would have told him.

'How about I get your uniform, Clementine, and you get changed in Dr Everingham's spare room?' her mother suggested.

Clementine looked from her mother to the doctor. The older man nodded. 'I think that's a very good idea.'

Clementine took a deep breath.

'All right, but only if we can go and talk to Miss Critchley straight away,' she replied.

'And you have to promise not to tell her what I told you.' Dr Everingham winked at Clementine. 'I don't want to get into trouble with my future daughter-in-law.'

Clementine slipped down from her chair and stood in front of the old man. 'Okay,' she said. 'I won't tell.'

A VERY BIG ANNOUNCEMENT

D r Everingham was right. About a lot of things. Clementine and her mother went straight to the office for a chat with Miss Critchley. The young woman listened and nodded and seemed to understand exactly what Clemmie was upset about. Miss Critchley asked Clementine and Lady Clarissa to wait a few minutes before they walked over to the classroom. She went ahead of them and by the time they arrived, the children were all sitting in different spots and there was an empty chair next to Sophie. Angus was beside another boy called Lester, who was the tallest in the class and seemed to wear a permanent frown on his face.

'Good morning, Clementine,' Miss Critchley greeted her at the door. 'I hear you've been to the doctor. I do hope you're feeling better.'

Clementine wondered why she said that when they had talked about it just a little while ago.

Mrs Bottomley strode over to where Clementine and her mother were standing. 'Well, I hope you're not sick. Kindergarten children are terribly good at spreading germs.' She frowned and a deep line ran down the middle of her forehead. 'I can tell you now that I am not in the mood for a bug.'

'Hello Mrs Bottomley, I'm Clemmie's mother, Clarissa Appleby.' She offered her hand.

The old woman smiled thinly and reluctantly reached out to take Clarissa's hand in hers.

'I can assure you that Clemmie's fine,' Lady Clarissa said as she looked at the teacher, who was dressed head to toe in beige.

'Good morning, Mrs Bottomley. That's a good suit. It would look nice with a red scarf,' Clementine suggested.

Mrs Bottomley didn't take kindly to the child's advice. 'I beg your pardon, young lady. I can't imagine ruining my beige with something as ghastly as red.'

'Oh, I think Clementine's absolutely right, Mrs Bottomley. A splash of red would look lovely,' Miss Critchley said, and winked at Clementine.

The teacher rolled her eyes.

'Look, Clementine, there's a spare spot next to Sophie,' said Miss Critchley, nodding at the empty desk. 'Would you like to sit there?'

Sophie was beaming and Clementine smiled back. 'Yes, please!'

'Bye bye, Clemmie, I'll see you after school.' Her mother gave her a quick hug and the girl ran to sit next to her friend.

'I'll walk you out,' Miss Critchley said to Lady Clarissa. 'And by the way, kindergarten, I have a lovely surprise for you later on at assembly.'

The class began to talk at once. 'Have a good day, Mrs Bottomley,' the head teacher said with a smile at the older woman.

Mrs Bottomley pursed her lips and nodded at Miss Critchley. 'All right, kindergarten, we need to focus.'

That morning, Clementine was astonished to realise that she had learned several words since the day before. When Mrs Bottomley asked for someone to read the sentence the class had written together on the board, Clemmie raised her hand. Of course Astrid raised hers first but this time Mrs Bottomley asked Clementine instead.

Clementine studied the squiggles carefully. 'It says …' She paused and concentrated hard, then read each word separately. '"I can play at school."'

'No, it says …' Mrs Bottomley looked at the board. 'Oh yes, I think you're actually right, Clementine.'

Sophie raised her hand. 'Is Clementine getting a sticker?' she asked.

Mrs Bottomley had just given Astrid three and then one to Angus because he recognised the word 'a'.

'Yes, I suppose so.' The teacher marched over to Clementine and placed a sticker on the collar of her uniform. It had a picture of a star on it and, Mrs Bottomley told her, the words said 'Well done'.

At morning tea time, Clemmie, Sophie and Poppy joined a game of chasings with half the class. Miss Critchley had called by their classroom just before they went out and asked Angus and Joshua if they could help her with some special jobs. They didn't come back to the classroom until after the bell had gone.

Lunchtime was better too. Miss Critchley came along to supervise and said that the children could sit with their friends. Clementine ate every last bite of her spaghetti bolognaise and the iceblock they were given for dessert.

After lunch they had assembly. Clementine was amazed to realise that she'd been so busy all day, she'd forgotten about Miss Critchley's surprise.

The smallest students were sitting on the floor at the front of the hall and the older children sat in rows behind them. The teachers perched on chairs around the edge of the room. Most of them were smiling, except Mrs Bottomley, who was trying to get Angus and the other boys at the end of her row to sit quietly.

Miss Critchley stood at the microphone. 'Good afternoon, everyone.'

'Goo-oodafternoo-ooonMissCritch-ley,' the group chorused in an echoey sing-song, which kindergarten struggled to keep up with.

'I hope you are all enjoying the new school term.'

Lots of children were nodding and smiling. Clementine noticed that most of the teachers were too.

'And I hope that you've settled in and are looking forward to the year ahead. Now, I have a very exciting announcement about a special day we're going to have next week.' Miss Critchley smiled at the group. 'I wonder if anyone would like to guess what we're doing.'

A sea of hands rose into the air.

'Yes, Jemima.' Miss Critchley pointed to a girl with brown plaits at the back of the room.

'Is it a kite day?' the child asked.

'I have a kite. It's blue,' a little boy in the front row called out. Everyone laughed.

Miss Critchley shook her head. 'That's a lovely idea, Jemima, but no, it's not a kite day.'

Hands shot back up again.

'Yes, Dougald.' She pointed at a boy in the middle of the group.

'Is it a cake stall?' he asked.

'My daddy makes cakes,' Sophie called and then put her hand over her mouth and giggled.

'He certainly does, Sophie,' Miss Critchley said. 'And they're delicious. But it's not a cake stall, although I think there might be some cakes on the day.'

Clementine raised her hand.

'Yes, Clementine,' said Miss Critchley with an extra-big smile.

'Is it a pet day?' Clementine asked.

'Hey, I told her that!' Angus yelled.

Mrs Bottomley glared at the boy and pulled sharply on his shirt collar.

Angus wrinkled his nose at his grandmother.

Lots of children began calling out about their pets. 'My dog's called Buster ... I've got a cat and he's called Nero ... my goldfish is the fastest swimmer ever ...'

'Settle down, everyone,' Miss Critchley commanded. 'Do you want to know if Clementine is right?'

The whole group nodded like performing seals.

'Yes, we're having a pet day.' Miss Critchley grinned at the excited group. 'On Monday. And there will be a whole lot of different competitions. Cutest pet, best dressed, most unusual, best tricks and lots more. We're supporting a charity called Queen Georgiana's Trust for the Protection of Animals. I'm sure that many of you know our wonderful queen is a lover of all creatures great and small. Through her trust she raises money to help look after abandoned pets. To enter your pet in the competition you'll have to bring a gold coin donation, which we will give to the trust.'

The children were squealing with excitement.

'Goodness, please calm down, everyone. I know it's terribly exciting,' called Miss Critchley.

'It's ghastly,' Mrs Bottomley muttered under her breath.

A small boy in the front row put up his hand.

The head teacher nodded at him. 'Yes, Riley.'

'Does it have to be a dog or a cat?' he asked.

'No, not at all. I know that some of you have quite unusual pets so I'm looking forward to seeing them all,' Miss Critchley replied.

Clementine was relieved to hear this. Surely she'd be able to bring Lavender.

Another hand went up.

'Yes Fergus,' she said, looking at a large lad at the back of the room.

'Can I bring Esteban?' he asked.

Miss Critchley raised her eyebrows. 'May I ask what Esteban is?'

'He's a python,' Fergus replied. 'But he's not poisonous.'

'I don't see why not, as long as he has a cage,' Miss Critchley nodded. 'And he's in it.'

Fergus had a smile from one ear to the other.

'But I don't like snakes,' Poppy said loudly.

Angus glared at her. 'Snakes are cool. And it will bite you because snakes don't like girls.'

'No, it won't,' Poppy retaliated.

'Angus Archibald!' shouted Miss Critchley. Her face was fierce. 'That wasn't nice at all. Please apologise to Poppy for frightening her.'

Angus gave Poppy a sulky 'sorry'. He looked as if he might cry. Mrs Bottomley looked cross.

There were more hands up.

'And I have another surprise,' Miss Critchley announced.

The front row of kindergarten children suddenly sat up straighter, as if a puppeteer was hovering above them and pulling their shoulders with invisible strings.

'We are very fortunate that Queen Georgiana herself will be here to judge the competition.'

The whole hall erupted with excited murmurs.

'All right, everyone. Settle down. There will be a note this afternoon with more details.'

'Mummy, I got a sticker.' Clementine beamed as she met her mother at the school gate and thrust her blazer lapel towards her. 'And Dr Everingham was right. Pet Day is next Monday and Lavender can come to school *all* day.'

Lady Clarissa hugged Clemmie tightly and planted a kiss on top of her head. 'It's nice to have my real daughter back again. I'm glad we got rid of that grumpy little imposter.'

'I love school, Mummy,' Clementine said.

'Well, I'm very pleased about that. You'd have been bored out of your mind if you had to stay at home with Uncle Digby and me for the rest of your days.' She could hardly believe the difference a day made. 'Guess who's back at home?' she asked.

'Aunt Violet?' Clementine guessed.

Lady Clarissa nodded. 'That's right. Shall we pop into Pierre's and get a lovely cake for afternoon tea? She might need some sweetening up.'

Clementine giggled. Her mother was probably right.

AUNT VIOLET

Clementine raced along the hallway and into the kitchen.

'Uncle Digby, Lavender, I got a sticker,' she called, grinning proudly.

Digby Pertwhistle was in the kitchen making a pot of tea. Clementine almost collided with him as he turned from the bench.

'Steady on, young lady,' Digby smiled at her. Clementine wrapped her arms around his middle. 'Sounds like school was much improved today.'

'Yes, it was wonderful. I got a sticker and we're having a pet day too,' Clementine fizzed.

Digby leaned down and whispered into Clemmie's ear. 'You might want to say hello to your Aunt Violet. She's sitting at the table.'

The child released the old man from her grip and ran towards Aunt Violet, who was surveying the scene with her crimson lips pursed.

'Hello Aunt Violet.' Clementine noticed that she was wearing a very stylish blue top over a pair of crisp white linen pants. 'I like your outfit. Did you have a good holiday?'

'Yes, it was ... splendid, actually,' the old woman said, as if she was surprised by her own answer.

'That's good. I hoped you'd come back in a better mood than when you left,' Clementine said.

Uncle Digby coughed.

'I mean, I hoped that all that time in the sea air would make you feel happier,' Clementine tried again.

'Really?' Her great-aunt shot her a frosty stare. 'Am I not a picture of contentment?'

Clementine wasn't sure what she meant but she nodded anyway.

'Pharaoh's been a good boy and he and Lavender love each other so much. You know they sleep in the same basket almost every night, except when Pharaoh sleeps down here in front of the stove. Sometimes he curls up on my pillow and he cuddles me,' Clementine prattled.

'Yes, well, he can come back to the Rose Room now,' Aunt Violet commented.

'But Mummy said that you're having the Blue Room up near me,' Clementine replied.

Lady Clarissa entered the kitchen. She'd been dragging Aunt Violet's luggage upstairs. The woman seemed to have enough clothes to start her own department store.

Aunt Violet looked at her niece. 'Is that true, Clarissa?'

Clarissa straightened her shoulders and looked her aunt right in the eye. 'I'm afraid,

Aunt Violet, that I need the Rose Room for paying guests. It's the best by far and the one I use to advertise the hotel. The Blue Room is perfectly lovely too and I've just bought a new duvet for your bed.'

'I don't know why you have to open *our* home to strangers,' the old woman scowled.

'Unless you'd like us all to be living in a tent on the Penberthy Floss Fields, that's something you're just going to have to get used to,' Clarissa replied. She looked towards Digby. He winked at her.

'But I don't want to share a bathroom,' Violet moaned. 'It's not … It's not civilised.'

'I'm afraid it's something we all have to do,' Clarissa replied. 'And it's hardly a great sacrifice.'

'But I'll have to share my bathroom with …' She paused and then sneered, 'the child.'

'It's all right, Aunt Violet. I don't take very long in there because I don't like the bathtub very much. It prickles my bottom. Mummy says that if she wins another bathroom makeover she'll get it fixed up but who knows when that will happen.'

Everyone knew about Lady Clarissa's love of competitions. She entered loads of them and had an uncanny knack for winning too. Over the years she'd won everything from a new car to a kitchen makeover, white goods and most recently a three-month round-the-world cruise, from which Aunt Violet had just returned.

'Well, I suppose the Blue Room will have to do,' Aunt Violet huffed.

'It will be fun, Aunt Violet,' Clementine commented. 'I can come and visit you with Lavender.'

'For heaven's sake, don't bring that pig anywhere near me, or my room,' Aunt Violet retorted.

'But if you get to know her, I'm sure that you'll love Lavender as much as I do, and Pharaoh adores her.' Clementine leaned down under the table. 'I think she likes you anyway,' she said, popping her head back up, 'because she's under your chair.'

Aunt Violet's feet shot off the floor so her legs stuck straight out.

'Remove the pig this minute!' she demanded.

Clementine put a finger to her lips. 'Shh. Lavender's asleep and she doesn't like being woken up when she's having her afternoon nap. She doesn't bite, you know.'

Aunt Violet simply said 'hmmph' and turned to Pharoah, who was preening himself at the back door. 'Come here, precious,' she called.

Pharaoh strolled across the kitchen floor, stopped at Aunt Violet's feet and stared up at her.

Aunt Violet relaxed her ridiculous pose and patted her lap.

Pharaoh studied his mistress for another moment. Then he flicked his tail and padded to the other side of the table where he leapt into Clementine's lap. He nuzzled her face and began to purr like a sports car engine.

'I see,' Aunt Violet harrumphed. 'That's where I stand these days.'

'He always sits in my lap at afternoon tea

time,' Clementine said. The cat kneaded her legs like bread dough before finding a comfortable position.

'I hope you haven't brainwashed him to forget me,' Aunt Violet said.

Clementine frowned. She'd never heard of anyone washing their brain before. 'Are you going to bring him to the pet day?' she asked. 'I'm taking Lavender and I'm going to enter her in everything.'

'I hardly think so.' Aunt Violet shook her head. 'Pharaoh's far too precious to mix with the village riffraff.'

'But we're giving the money to Queen Georgiana's animals.'

At the mention of Queen Georgiana's name, Violet's ears pricked up. 'Will she be there?'

'Oh, yes. Miss Critchley said that she's coming to judge the competition,' Clementine replied. 'That was part of the big surprise and the reason we have to have the pet day so soon.'

'Fancy that,' said Uncle Digby. 'You've always

wanted to meet her, haven't you, Miss Appleby. Didn't you invite her to a party once?'

Aunt Violet eyeballed him. 'Of course not, Pertwhistle, don't be so ridiculous.'

'I can't wait to meet her,' said Clementine. 'I'm going to practise my curtseys. And I'm going to teach Lavender how to curtsey too.'

'What a lot of nonsense,' Aunt Violet snapped. 'Now hurry up and pour that tea before it's stone cold.'

Lady Clarissa exchanged a puzzled look with Digby.

'So,' said Aunt Violet before either of them could speak. 'You must tell me, Clarissa, are there any ghastly guests booked in to stay here over the weekend?'

SCHOOL DAYS

The rest of the week whizzed past and Clementine continued to enjoy her days at school. Poppy and Sophie and Clemmie spent lunchtimes playing games on the field. Even Angus seemed to be better behaved, although he and Joshua did spend a lot of time helping Miss Critchley with jobs. One lunchtime, Angus tried to convince Clemmie that Queen Georgiana hated pigs, but she decided it was best not to believe him.

Every night, Clemmie brought home a reader

and would practise at the kitchen table with Uncle Digby or her mother. She had even convinced Aunt Violet to listen to her one evening.

'Seriously, that must be the most boring tripe I've ever heard, Clementine. Can't you bring home some proper stories?' the old woman had complained before trotting off to the library. She'd returned with a dusty book called *A Little Princess*, by Frances Hodgson Burnett.

Clementine had asked if she was going to read it to her.

'Heavens, no.' Aunt Violet had shaken her head. 'But this is what you should be aiming to read. A proper story.'

The book had sat on the kitchen sideboard for the rest of the week, just begging to be opened.

On Saturday afternoon, Lady Clarissa and Digby Pertwhistle were busy attending to three guests who had booked in for the weekend at the very last minute. Clementine and Lavender were in the kitchen having a snack when Aunt Violet appeared.

'Hello Aunt Violet,' Clementine smiled at her.

The old woman was dressed in a smart pair of navy pants and a white blouse.

Clementine studied her outfit. 'You look nice.'

'Yes, well.' Aunt Violet considered Clementine's own choice of a pretty pink dress with white polka dots. 'Your dress is ... sweet.'

'Thank you, Aunt Violet,' said Clementine.

Aunt Violet went to the sink, filled the kettle with water and popped it on the stove.

'Grandpa's glad that you're here,' said Clementine, looking up from her chocolate brownie.

Aunt Violet spun around. 'Clementine, that's nonsense. Your grandfather has been dead for years and I'm sure that he couldn't care less whether I'm here or not.'

Clementine shook her head stubbornly. 'That's not true. I was talking to Granny and Grandpa this morning and they are both very happy that you're home.'

Aunt Violet seemed puzzled. 'Do you really think so?'

'Oh, yes.' Clemmie's head jiggled up and down.

Aunt Violet finished making her tea, carried it over to the table and sat down.

Clementine slipped off the chair and returned to the table clutching the book Aunt Violet had left on the sideboard.

'Could you read to me?' She stood in front of the old woman, looking up at her piercing ink-blue eyes.

Aunt Violet shooed her away. 'I'm busy, Clementine.'

'No, you're not. You're having a cup of tea,' Clementine insisted. 'That's not busy.'

'Well, I don't want to then,' Aunt Violet snapped.

Clementine's eyes began to cloud over.

'Oh, for goodness sake, it's nothing to cry about.' Aunt Violet placed the teacup down on the saucer with a thud. 'Give it to me.' She snatched the book from Clementine's hand.

'And sit down there.' She pointed at the seat next to her.

Clementine scurried up onto the chair. Pharaoh had made himself comfortable in the basket in front of the stove, where it was toasty and warm. Lavender hopped up from where she was sitting under the table and waddled over to join her friend.

Violet Appleby opened the book and scanned the inscription on the first page.

To our dearest Violet,
On the occasion of your sixth birthday,
Your loving Mama and Papa
xoxo

Something caught in Aunt Violet's throat and she turned the page before Clementine could see what she was looking at. She began to read.

Clementine sat wide-eyed as her great-aunt turned the pages and the story came to life right in front of her. Neither of them realised that a whole hour had passed.

Lady Clarissa appeared in the kitchen carrying an empty tea tray.

'Hello, what do we have here?' she enquired.

Aunt Violet snapped the book shut.

'Please don't stop, Aunt Violet,' Clementine begged.

'I have things to do, Clementine. I can't sit around here all day, can I?' The old woman stood and strode out of the room.

Clementine was confused. 'Did I do something wrong?' she asked her mother.

'No, Clemmie,' Lady Clarissa said, shaking her head. 'Aunt Violet can be a bit of a puzzle, that's all.'

Clementine nodded. 'She's much harder to work out than the ones we do at school.'

PET
DAY

'A re you *really* not coming with us, Aunt Violet?' Clementine asked her great-aunt at breakfast on Monday morning. 'It's not too late to enter Pharaoh in a competition.'

Violet looked up from the toast she was buttering. 'No Clementine, I won't be attending and neither will Pharaoh,' she said firmly.

Lady Clarissa glanced at the clock on the kitchen wall. 'Clemmie, you'd better run up and get Lavender ready,' she advised. 'We'll be leaving in half an hour.'

'She's so excited, Mummy. I'm taking her tutu and ballet slippers for the dress-up competition,' Clementine babbled.

Aunt Violet rolled her eyes. 'I almost feel sorry for the ridiculous creature. A pig in a tutu is too, too much.'

Clarissa laughed at her aunt's accidental joke.

'Oh no, Aunt Violet, Lavender loves to dress up. Mrs Mogg makes her clothes too,' said Clementine. She gave her mother a quick hug and sped off down the hallway.

'Are you sure you won't come along?' Lady Clarissa asked her aunt. 'It's bound to be lots of fun.'

'No, I'd rather eat cold brussels sprouts,' Aunt Violet said with a shudder.

'Well, if you change your mind, you're very welcome.' Clarissa stood up to clear the breakfast things. Digby Pertwhistle arrived in the room carrying a feather duster and cloth.

He'd been up early to get a head start on some of the housework. 'You're coming, aren't you?' Clarissa asked the old man.

'I wouldn't miss it for the world. Clemmie's so excited and I think Queen Georgiana's fabulous.' He winked at Aunt Violet.

Aunt Violet glared back.

An hour later the house was strangely silent. Aunt Violet was rattling around in her room when she decided to make herself some tea. As she descended the stairs she noticed a small black bag on the floor in the entrance hall. She marched over to pick it up and saw some pink tulle poking out.

She opened the bag to have a better look and found a pink collar and lead and a floral garland among the tiny tutu and four ballet slippers.

'Urgh, it belongs to the pig,' she exclaimed. She stuffed the contents back inside the bag and placed it on the hall table.

A moment later, a loose window shutter banged upstairs and Aunt Violet leapt into the air. She looked up towards the noise and locked eyes with her brother – or at least, the portrait of him hanging on the wall.

'What are you looking at, Edmund?' She didn't like the way his eyes seemed to be following her. 'No, I'm not going,' she said decisively.

Aunt Violet shook her head. Obviously she'd been spending too much time with the little one, who believed that the portraits could speak to her. And besides, she was far too busy to go running into town for a silly pet show.

Aunt Violet stalked off to the kitchen to make her tea. But all the while there was a gnawing feeling in her stomach. She caught sight of the book she'd been reading with Clementine. She'd forgotten how much she had loved that story. She smiled to herself as she recalled sitting with her mother on the veranda many years ago. They'd been reading the exact same book and Violet's beloved little terrier Hinchley was curled up on her lap. How she had loved that dog.

'Oh, all right, I'm going,' she muttered under her breath, before removing the kettle from the stovetop. She scurried up the back stairs to her bedroom, where she retrieved her handbag and car keys. Coming down the main stairs, she spotted Pharaoh through the double doors to the right. He was lying on the sitting room floor, basking in a shard of sunlight.

Aunt Violet looked back at her brother. 'Are you happy now?' She picked up the bag from the table. Checking that she had her house keys, the old woman strode to the front door. Her shiny red car was parked in the turning circle. She locked the house, walked over to the vehicle and opened the driver's side door before she realised that she'd left her sunglasses on the dresser in her bedroom. Aunt Violet sighed deeply and shook her head, tutting at herself.

She headed back inside, leaving the door ajar. As she climbed the stairs, she didn't notice a grey streak race out the door and towards the car.

Within a minute, Aunt Violet was speeding towards Highton Mill, the black bag on the passenger seat and her sunglasses perched on her nose.

THE BIG
MOMENT

'And who do we have here?' Queen Georgiana asked Clementine. She smiled at Lavender. The pig looked up at the old woman and seemed to smile back at her. The Queen was currently judging the Cutest Pet category inside the school hall. Queen Georgiana's lady-in-waiting, a stout woman of advanced years, was following closely behind. The woman wore a suit like those preferred by Mrs Bottomley and she had a snarl on her face to match.

Clementine curtsied just as Miss Critchley had taught the girls, and then replied, 'Her name is Lavender, Your Majesty, and she's a teacup.' Clementine giggled. 'I mean a teacup pig.'

'And so she is.' Queen Georgiana reached out to give Lavender a scratch behind the ear. 'And a very pretty little piggy you are too.' Lavender sniffed the Queen's hand before giving her finger a nibble. 'Oh, you cheeky thing,' she gasped and laughed loudly.

Her lady-in-waiting screwed up her nose and whispered under her breath, 'How ghastly. A pig!'

Queen Georgiana's ears pricked up. So did Clementine's.

'For heaven's sake, Mrs Marmalade, this piggy is so clean you could eat your dinner off her belly.'

Clementine smothered a giggle as she imagined Lavender acting as the Queen's dinner plate.

Mrs Marmalade sniffed and muttered a half-hearted apology to Clementine.

The Queen continued along the line. Sophie was standing beside Clementine and holding her cat Mintie, who was wriggling like a garden worm. Sophie curtsied too and almost lost her grip on the ball of white fur.

'If I were you, dear, I'd pop her into that cage there,' the Queen suggested, 'before she gets away. I don't like the look of that dog over there one little bit.' She nodded towards a giant mastiff who was drooling all over the floor. Standing beside the dog was its owner, Angus, who had a very loose grip on the lead. 'I don't know if that boy would be strong enough to hold the pup if something took his fancy.'

Sophie nodded. She wanted to say something but the words just wouldn't come out.

The Queen looked at the silent girl closely. 'Are you all right?'

Sophie nodded again.

'I don't bite, you know,' the Queen grinned.

Sophie nodded for a third time and was very cross with herself.

There were only a couple more pets at the

end of the line, including Esteban, Fergus's python. When Queen Georgiana reached him she stooped lower to make eye contact. Mrs Marmalade stepped away from the creature with a look of horror.

'Good grief, Marmalade, it's a python not a viper. Cute as a button too.' The Queen touched the serpent on the end of his scaly nose.

Fergus grinned broadly.

Mrs Marmalade shuddered.

The Queen concluded her inspections and moved over to confer with Miss Critchley, who was holding a blue ribbon.

There was a lot of nodding and smiling between them before Queen Georgiana took the microphone. 'It gives me great pleasure to announce that the Cutest Pet at today's Ellery Prep Pet Day is …' There was a long pause as the Queen cast her eye over the entrants one last time.

The audience members all held their breath.

'I must tell you that it was a terribly difficult decision and if I had my way everyone would take home a ribbon,' said Queen Georgiana, smiling at the children.

The audience exhaled, as if a room full of balloons had been let down at once.

'But, alas, there can only be one winner.' The group breathed in again. 'And today that title belongs to … Mintie the lovely little white cat.'

Everyone clapped. Sophie couldn't believe it. Her jaw dropped and her mouth gaped open like a stunned cod. She had been quite sure that Lavender would win.

'Sophie, close your mouth,' her father Pierre called from the audience, 'or you will catch some flies.' Everyone laughed.

Clementine smiled at her friend, and then leaned down and gave Lavender a pat. 'There's still the Best Dressed,' she whispered. 'And you'll look beautiful in your ballet slippers.'

Queen Georgiana strode over to Sophie, who was busy pulling Mintie out of her cage. The Queen pinned the oversized rosette onto the cat's collar. Mintie immediately started tearing at it with her teeth. Flashes were going off as Pierre snapped pictures of his daughter and her prize-winning cat standing next to the Queen.

'Would you like to say anything, dear?' Queen Georgiana held out the microphone to the astounded child.

Sophie could only manage to shake her head.

'I see the cat's still got your tongue.' Queen Georgiana winked at Sophie.

Mintie meowed loudly. It sounded rather like 'thank you'. The audience giggled.

Sophie's cheeks turned bright red.

'Thank you, Your Majesty,' she whispered.

'You're very welcome, my dear. Now put that kitty away again quick smart.' The Queen glared at Angus and his hound, who had moved to the front row. She wondered if he was entered in the next category: Dribbliest Pet.

Meanwhile, outside, Aunt Violet screeched to a halt at the front gate. She gathered up the black bag on the seat beside her and opened the driver's door, failing to see the 'No parking' sign right beside her car.

'Silly child would forget her head if it wasn't screwed on,' she tutted under her breath.

Digby Pertwhistle was outside helping set up the morning tea. He spotted the old woman exiting her car and scurried to meet her.

'Good morning, Miss Appleby, I see you changed your mind.'

'No, I did not.' Aunt Violet peered over the roof of her expensive red car. She didn't notice the shadow that scurried underneath the vehicle.

'May I ask what you're doing here then?' said the old man.

'I have this.' Aunt Violet held the bag aloft. She slammed the car door.

'Oh, it's very good of you to bring Clementine's bag. I don't think she realised that it was missing. But you can't park here,' he said, pointing at the sign.

'Pooh! I'll only be a minute,' she said, waving her hand at him.

'Well, I can take the bag for you and then

you don't need to come in at all,' Digby offered.

Aunt Violet shook her head. 'No, I'll take it myself.' She pursed her lips together tightly. 'I want Clementine to understand that she has to be more careful with her things. She can't expect someone to rescue her every time she's careless.'

'Oh,' said Digby. 'Of course. She is five, after all. I don't suppose it has anything to do with you wanting to meet Queen Georgiana?'

'Of course not,' Aunt Violet snapped.

'You're not even a little curious?' Digby teased.

'No.' She shook her head.

'Well, I think you'll find Clementine over in the hall with the rest of the children. The Best Dressed category will be coming up soon. Then you might like to stay for morning tea – after you've moved the car, of course.'

Violet ignored Digby's last comment and marched through the gates. She almost bumped into Clementine and Lavender, who were on their way to the classroom to get ready. Mrs Bottomley was leading the group – in a straight line, of course. Her mouth was pinched and her eyebrows looked crosser than ever. She was not enjoying Pet Day one little bit, although the layered sponge cake she'd made for the event had been a great triumph, so she had that to look forward to at morning tea.

'Aunt Violet!' Clementine exclaimed. 'I'm glad you changed your mind.'

'I did no such thing,' the woman snarled. She held the black bag aloft. 'You forgot this.'

'Oh, thank you for bringing it. Otherwise we would have missed out.' Clementine smiled at her great-aunt. She hadn't even realised that the bag was missing.

'Well, yes, you need to be more careful in future, Clementine. I can't go running around after you at the drop of a hat,' said Aunt Violet. She looked as if she had just sucked a lemon.

'Thank you, Aunt Violet,' Clementine said again. 'Are you going to stay for the judging?' Clementine asked.

'No, I'm going home to make another cup of tea. The one I was trying to make when your grandfather scolded me about your bag will be stone cold,' Aunt Violet replied.

'Did Grandpa talk to you too? That's so exciting!' Clementine gushed.

'No, of course he did not talk to me,' said Aunt Violet. 'I didn't mean it like that at all.'

But Clementine knew there was something more. She gave Aunt Violet a wave and skipped along with Lavender beside her on the way to the classroom.

Inside the hall, there were peals of laughter as Queen Georgiana announced the winner of the Dribbliest Pet category.

It was a tie. Father Bob had kindly loaned his bulldog, Adrian, to Eddie Whipple, a six-year-old lad from Penberthy Floss. The other winner was Angus's giant mastiff, Martin. The Queen was calling for a mop to clean the stage before the next category, Best Dressed.

Aunt Violet was drawn towards the noise and wondered what on earth was going on. She poked her head into the back of the hall and watched as Her Majesty directed the school caretaker, Quentin Pickles, who was slipping and sliding all over the place.

'Come on, man.' Queen Georgiana pointed at a pool on the stage. 'You missed a bit just there.' The audience was hooting.

'Oh, for goodness sake, give it to me.' Her Majesty wrestled the mop from Mr Pickles, whose face had turned a stony white.

'But, Ma'am, you're the Queen. You can't mop floors. That's my job,' the old man protested, clutching the mop back to his chest.

'Yes, you're quite right. I am the Queen, so I can jolly well do anything I please.' Queen Georgiana flashed him a cheeky grin.

The parents and children wondered if they were watching a pantomime.

Violet Appleby pursed her lips. Could this really be the Queen? The very same woman she had invited to her birthday party when they were girls, and from whom she never received a reply?

Outside, Digby and Pierre were putting the finishing touches to the morning tea. A row of trestle tables heaved under the weight of cream buns, chocolate eclairs, sponge cakes and a scrumptious selection of biscuits and slices. Most had been supplied by Pierre, with some additions from the parents and teachers.

'Well come on, Pierre,' Digby called to his friend. 'We should be getting in. I think Clementine and Lavender are about to be judged.'

The two men placed a long gauze cover over the tables and headed inside.

Clementine Rose and Lavender – now in her costume – followed Mrs Bottomley around to the side entrance of the hall.

'Okay, Lavender, just do your best.' Clementine reached down and gave the little pig a scratch behind the ear. She walked across the stage and was joined by a whole line of children and their pets, which were dressed in a range of outfits. There was a West Highland terrier in a sailor suit, a bunny dressed as a bellhop and, of course, Lavender in her tutu. Poppy was there too with one of the barn cats from their farm. It was a large tabby called Jezabel, dressed in a bride's outfit that Poppy had borrowed from one of her dolls. Jezabel did not look as if she was enjoying the experience one little bit.

'Oh my,' Queen Georgiana gasped as she surveyed the group in front of her. 'Don't you all look gorgeous?'

She walked up and down the line, greeting the pets and their owners. Digby slid into a seat next to Lady Clarissa. He glanced around and saw Aunt Violet standing at the back of the hall. He motioned for her to come and sit down but she ignored him completely.

After a short deliberation, Queen Georgiana again took the microphone from Miss Critchley to announce the winner.

'It gives me great pleasure to award the Best Dressed pet to ... Lavender, the little teacup pig.' She smiled at Clementine, who beamed back at her.

'That's our girl,' Digby called from the back of the hall. Everyone clapped and laughed.

Queen Georgiana passed the microphone back to Miss Critchley and proceeded to pin the blue rosette onto Lavender's tutu. The little pig nibbled Her Majesty's finger and Clementine curtsied.

DISASTER

'Well,' Miss Critchley began, 'I can't believe it's time for our final category: the Pet Most Like its Owner.'

All of the students and their pets, other than those entered in the last section, were now jammed in together at the front of the hall with parents and friends sitting on the rows of seats behind.

'I love this part of the competition,' Miss Critchley beamed. 'It's always a lot of fun.

So, without any further ado, here are the entrants.'

The children and their pets filed across the stage. Among them were a girl from the fourth grade with blonde curls and her equally blonde curly-haired poodle; a lad from the sixth grade with slicked back hair holding a large skink in a terrarium; and a kindergarten boy with rather large ears, who was leading a basset hound. Another boy was wearing a dalmatian costume and holding the most adorable dalmatian puppy. Queen Georgiana was grinning broadly as she tried to decide on a winner.

No one noticed the unusual creature that had slunk onto the side of the stage. He padded along behind the group and emerged in the middle, between a girl with a guinea pig and a lad with a ferret.

The creature looked out at the audience with a sneer on its face.

Queen Georgiana caught her breath. 'Oh my. Who do we have here?'

A little girl in the front row squealed, 'There's a monster. There's a monster.'

'Good lord, what is that?' a man asked loudly from the middle of the hall.

The father with the dragon tattoo leapt to his feet and said, 'Quick, get a cage before it bites someone and they turn into an alien too. I've read about those creatures. It's dangerous for sure.'

Several of the parents charged forward. One of them grabbed a blanket from a toddler who was sitting with his mother. The little boy began to wail.

From the back of the hall, Aunt Violet caught sight of the commotion and gasped. Clementine did too. Lavender grunted.

'Pharaoh! My baby!' Aunt Violet exclaimed. 'How on earth did you get here?' The old woman rushed down the centre of the hall, sending children scattering this way and that. She elbowed the men who were racing towards the stage.

'Get away from him,' Aunt Violet roared. 'Do not lay a hand on my baby or I'll ...'

'Ah!' yelled one of the men as he caught sight of Aunt Violet's angry face. She was far more petrifying than the creature on the stage.

A little girl began to cry. 'Mummy,' she sobbed, 'there's a witch.'

'No, that's just Aunt Violet. She always looks like that,' Clementine called in her great-aunt's defence.

Aunt Violet reached the stage and pushed her way to the middle, where she scooped the cat into her arms. He looked at her and hissed.

'What are you all looking at?' she challenged the audience, who were now staring wide-eyed at the terrifying woman and her equally terrifying pet.

'What *is* that?' a lady called from the back row.

'He's a sphynx, you ridiculous woman. Everyone knows that,' Aunt Violet hissed.

The audience members looked at one another and shrugged.

'He's lovely. You just have to get to know him, that's all,' Clementine announced.

'He's ugly, did you say?' a man shouted.

As always, Queen Georgiana knew just how to break the tension.

'I see we have a last-minute entrant,' she said, nodding at Aunt Violet and then turning to face the audience, who laughed loudly.

Digby Pertwhistle leaned over to Lady Clarissa and whispered in her ear. 'It looks like she'll finally get her wish.'

Clarissa nodded, although she was feeling a little sorry for Aunt Violet.

'To meet the Queen,' Digby said.

'Oh,' Clarissa nodded.

'I wonder how Pharaoh got here,' Clementine said to Poppy and Sophie, who were sitting either side of her.

'I don't know, but your Aunt Violet doesn't look very happy,' Sophie replied.

'Aunt Violet never looks very happy,' Clementine said.

Aunt Violet stood on the stage, staring at the audience and wondering what they were giggling about. The cat hissed at her again.

Aunt Violet sneered and hissed back at him. The audience hooted with laughter and so did Queen Georgiana.

In her light grey suit and oversized sunglasses, Aunt Violet bore more than a passing resemblance to Pharaoh.

'I think we have our winner,' Her Majesty declared. She took the blue rosette from the tray Mrs Marmalade was carrying behind her. 'Excuse me, dear, do you know that lady's name?' Queen Georgiana whispered to Miss Critchley, who shook her head.

'But we're not …' Violet began to protest. 'You couldn't possibly think …'

'And the winner of the Pet Most Like its Owner goes to –' Queen Georgiana turned towards Aunt Violet and looked at the cat. 'Well, what's his name?'

Violet gulped. 'Pharaoh,' she whispered.

'And the winner is Pharaoh and his owner,' Queen Georgiana announced. The audience went wild.

ESCAPE ARTIST

'That was fun.' Clementine beamed at her mother and Uncle Digby as they ate their morning tea outside. 'I'm so proud of Lavender and Pharaoh and Aunt Violet too.'

Her great-aunt did not feel the same way at all. She had been standing behind a tree, quietly nibbling a piece of Pierre's delicious chocolate cake and doing her best to stay out of sight. But she'd been cornered by Father Bob, who'd come to collect Adrian, his dribbly bulldog. He was congratulating her loudly on the win with

Pharaoh, who was now safely locked away in a spare cat cage that Miss Critchley had found. Violet was protesting that it was all just a ridiculous mistake. Father Bob didn't agree. He thought it was well deserved.

'Who would have thought Aunt Violet and Pharaoh would be such a hit?' said Digby. He winked at Clementine.

'Do you think we could invite Queen Georgiana to tea?' Clementine asked. 'I like her a lot.'

'Yes, the woman has impeccable judgement,' Digby grinned.

'I'm not sure that Aunt Violet would want that,' Lady Clarissa replied. She glanced towards the cake table, where something caught her eye. 'No, Pharaoh!' she shouted and ran towards him.

Aunt Violet and Father Bob looked up.

Hiding behind a huge layered sponge in the middle of the table was Pharaoh. His tail flicked from side to side like a windscreen wiper as he licked the cream from between the cakes.

Mrs Bottomley had been telling Astrid's

parents what a clever little tick their daughter was, when she heard the commotion too.

She looked up, wondering if she was seeing things.

'Why, you!' Mrs Bottomley erupted. 'I spent hours making that cake, you ugly brute.' She raced towards the table and lunged at the cat. Pharaoh darted away and Mrs Bottomley landed sprawled out, face down in the middle of the sponge.

Clementine's eyes were like saucers as she watched her teacher lying on the table with her little brown legs kicking in the air.

Aunt Violet threw her paper plate on the ground. Pharaoh raced in her direction. She quickly snatched him up but the evidence was all over his face.

Mrs Bottomley rocked backward until her feet hit the ground and she slid off the table and onto her bottom. Large chunks of cake fell from her chest as she scrambled to her feet and sped towards Aunt Violet, who was clutching Pharaoh under her arm.

'You, you horrid little beast!' Mrs Bottomley pointed her finger at the cat. Although the teacher was trembling like a jelly, Clementine marvelled that her helmet of brown curls barely moved.

'Someone must have let him out,' stammered Aunt Violet. She was looking in the direction of Pharaoh's cage and wondering which of those ghastly children had done it. Angus Archibald was standing beside the cage with Joshua, giggling behind his hands. 'It was you,' Aunt Violet hissed as she stalked towards the two boys.

Angus pulled a face. 'Was not.'

'We didn't do anything,' Joshua said and started to laugh. He was looking at the bits of pink icing stuck to Mrs Bottomley's face.

'My grandson would never do any such thing,' said Mrs Bottomley. She marched over to Aunt Violet. 'I'm sure it was ... Clementine and her naughty little friends!'

Clementine frowned. She'd been standing beside Uncle Digby and her mother the whole time and Poppy and Sophie weren't even there.

Unfortunately for Mrs Bottomley, Angus had reached down to the ground just moments before and picked up the pin from the latch on the cage. He was still holding it in his hand. She saw it with her own eyes.

'Oh!' Mrs Bottomley gasped. Her bottom lip began to tremble. 'Angus Archibald!' she roared, and then started to cry.

'But I didn't do anything.' Angus shook his head and then looked at the evidence in his hand. 'It wasn't me. I just found this on the ground.'

Aunt Violet spun around and glared at the teacher. 'Ha! If I were you, madam, I would be a little more careful about accusing my great-niece in future, especially when your grandson is quite clearly the troublemaker. And what on earth are you wearing? Perhaps no one has ever been kind enough to say so, but brown is definitely not your colour!'

'How dare you?' Ethel Bottomley poked her tongue out at Aunt Violet and scurried away. Lady Clarissa raced after her. She couldn't believe what Aunt Violet had said, even if they might all have been thinking it. Angus and Joshua were wide eyed – at least for a second, until Aunt Violet got stuck into the pair of them. Once she had finished yelling, they both made a hasty exit, wiping their eyes as they went.

Aunt Violet let out an enormous sigh. As far as she was concerned the day couldn't possibly get any worse. But she hadn't noticed Queen Georgiana walking towards her.

'Oh my goodness, dear, if I didn't think you looked alike before, you certainly do now,' the Queen said with a grin.

'I don't know what you mean, Ma'am.' Violet gulped and clutched Pharaoh closer to her chest.

Queen Georgiana touched the corner of her own lip with her forefinger.

Violet wondered what she was doing.

Clementine rushed over with Lavender in tow. She pointed at Aunt Violet's face and passed her a tissue.

'What? What's the matter now?' Violet asked.

'Your lip, dear. It's covered in cream,' Queen Georgiana smiled. 'Just like that naughty little fiend.' She pointed at Pharaoh.

'Oh. Thank you,' Violet mumbled and wiped her face.

Queen Georgiana was ushered away by her bodyguard and lady-in-waiting.

'Would you like to go home, Aunt Violet?' Clementine asked. 'Lavender's exhausted. And Pharaoh looks as if he could do with a nap too.'

'Yes, I'm going right now,' Aunt Violet fumed and began to stride away.

'Can I come with you?' Clementine called. 'Mummy and Uncle Digby are staying to help clean up and I thought we could read some more of that story.'

But Aunt Violet was in no mood to babysit. 'No. I'm taking Pharaoh and you're not coming.'

Clementine frowned. Uncle Digby had disappeared inside and Sophie and Poppy were nowhere to be seen either. Her mother was near the entrance to the hall, still trying to calm Mrs Bottomley.

Clemmie hadn't noticed Angus Archibald skulking around behind her.

'You – love – a – pig,' Angus sniffled.

'Go away, Angus,' Clementine replied. 'You've made enough trouble.' She spun around to face the lad. It was obvious he'd been crying. She almost felt sorry for him.

'I didn't do it,' Angus protested. 'I didn't.'

Clementine wondered if maybe he was telling the truth. He had been a lot better the past few days.

'Where's your dog?' Clementine asked.

'Mum took him and I have to stay here and help clean up,' Angus explained between sniffs. 'Then I have to go to Nan's and she's really mad.'

'Well, you shouldn't have let Pharaoh out,' Clementine admonished. 'Aunt Violet is really cross with you too.'

'But I told you. I didn't,' Angus huffed. 'I found that pin on the ground.'

The boy stared at Lavender, who was munching on some cake that Mrs Bottomley had scraped from her chest at the height of the drama. The little pig looked up at the boy.

'Can I pat her?' Angus asked Clementine.

'Yes, but you have to promise to be gentle,' Clemmie replied.

The lad knelt down and gave the little pig a scratch behind her ear. She pressed her snout against his other hand and gave him a nibble.

Angus giggled. 'That tickles.'

'See, she's really lovely,' Clementine said. 'And she likes you.'

Angus didn't notice the shadow looming over them, blocking out the sun. When finally he glanced up, his face crumpled and he raced off to put a safe distance between him and Clementine's terrifying great-aunt.

'Well, are you coming or not?' Aunt Violet had deposited Pharaoh into the car and returned to the scene of the crime.

The child smiled up at her. 'Oh, yes please,' Clementine said. 'You take Lavender and I'll just find Mummy and Uncle Digby and let them know I'm going with you.' She thrust the pig into Aunt Violet's arms.

The old woman flinched. She held Lavender out in front of her and the little pig kicked her legs about. Aunt Violet walked back to the car, where she placed Lavender on the back seat beside Pharaoh, who was locked up in his borrowed cage.

A minute later Clementine appeared. 'I'm ready.' She hopped into the passenger seat and closed the door. 'Mummy said that she and Uncle Digby will be home soon.'

Aunt Violet started the car. 'I'm not reading anything until I've had a strong cup of tea and a lie down,' she announced.

'But you didn't say you wouldn't read to me at all,' Clementine smiled.

Aunt Violet said nothing. She simply put the car into gear and pulled away from the kerb.

Clementine turned her head to look at the animals in the back. She was surprised to see Pharaoh curled up on the seat beside Lavender.

'Aunt Violet, did you lock Pharaoh in the cage?' the child asked.

'Of course I did.' The woman kept her eyes firmly on the road ahead. 'I latched it myself.'

'Well, it's just … I think you might have to apologise to Angus,' Clementine began.

'I'll do no such thing,' Aunt Violet retorted.

'I think you should,' Clementine insisted.

'Why?' Aunt Violet snapped.

'Because Pharoah's a magician,' the child said, frowning. If she didn't know better, she would have sworn that Pharaoh was smiling.

CAST OF CHARACTERS

The Appleby household

Clementine Rose Appleby   Five-year-old daughter of Lady Clarissa

Lavender   Clemmie's teacup pig

Lady Clarissa Appleby   Clementine's mother and the owner of Penberthy House

Digby Pertwhistle   Butler at Penberthy House

Aunt Violet Appleby	Clementine's grandfather's sister
Pharaoh	Aunt Violet's beloved sphynx

Friends and village folk

Margaret Mogg	Owner of the Penberthy Floss village shop
Father Bob	Village minister
Adrian	Father Bob's dribbly bulldog
Pierre Rousseau	Owner of Pierre's Patisserie in Highton Mill
Odette Rousseau	Wife of Pierre and mother of Jules and Sophie
Jules Rousseau	Seven-year-old brother of Sophie
Sophie Rousseau	Clementine's best friend – also five years old
Mintie	Sophie's white kitten
Poppy Bauer	Clementine's friend who lives on the farm at Highton Hall

Jasper Bauer	Poppy's older brother
Lily Bauer	Poppy and Jasper's mother

School staff and students

Miss Arabella Critchley	Head teacher at Ellery Prep
Mrs Ethel Bottomley	Teacher at Ellery Prep
Quentin Pickles	Caretaker
Mrs Winky	Dinner lady
Angus Archibald	Naughty kindergarten boy
Joshua	Friend of Angus's
Astrid	Clever kindergarten girl

Others

Dr Everingham	Clementine's family doctor
Daisy Rumble	Doctor's temp receptionist

ABOUT
THE AUTHOR

Jacqueline Harvey taught for many years in girls' boarding schools. She is the author of the bestselling Alice-Miranda series and the Clementine Rose series, and was awarded Honour Book in the 2006 Australian CBC Awards for her picture book *The Sound of the Sea*. She now writes full-time and is working on more Alice-Miranda and Clementine Rose adventures.

www.jacquelineharvey.com.au

Collect the series

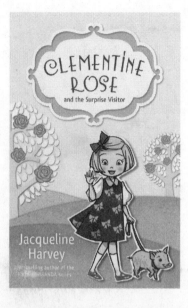